© 2004 Ann Arbor

About the Translators

ROBERT BLY's recent books of poetry include two books of *ghazals*, *My Sentence Was a Thousand Years of Joy* and *The Night Abraham Called to the Stars*. He has published his selected translations in *The Winged Energy of Delight* and has received many literary prizes, including the National Book Award. His prose works include *The Sibling Society*, *The Maiden King* (with Marion Woodman), and *Iron John*. His recent work *The Insanity of Empire* is a collection of poems against the war in Iraq.

DR. LEONARD LEWISOHN was a research associate in esotericism in Islam at the Department of Academic Research and Publications of the Institute of Ismaili Studies (London) from 1999 to 2005. He is Lecturer in Persian and the Iran Heritage Foundation Fellow in Classical Persian and Sufi Literature at the Institute of Arab and Islamic Studies at the University of Exeter in England. He is the author of *Beyond Faith and Infidelity* and has edited many studies of Sufi literature, including the three-volume *Heritage of Sufism* and *Attar and the Persian Sufi Tradition* (with Chistopher Shackle).

The Angels Knocking on the Tavern Door

ALSO BY ROBERT BLY

Poetry
Silence in the Snowy Fields
The Light Around the Body
The Man in the Black Coat Turns
Loving a Woman in Two Worlds
Meditations on the Insatiable Soul
Morning Poems
Eating the Honey of Words: New and Selected Poems
The Night Abraham Called to the Stars
My Sentence Was a Thousand Years of Joy

Anthologies
The Rag and Bone Shop of the Heart
    (with James Hillman and Michael Meade)
News of the Universe: Poems of Twofold Consciousness
The Soul Is Here for Its Own Joy

Prose
Talking All Morning (Interviews)
The Eight Stages of Translation
A Little Book on the Human Shadow (with William
    Booth)
Iron John: A Book About Men
The Sibling Society
*The Maiden King: The Reunion of Masculine and
    Feminine* (with Marion Woodman)

Translations
The Winged Energy of Delight: Selected Translations
Selected Poems of Rainer Maria Rilke
Times Alone: Selected Poems of Antonio Machado
Neruda and Vallejo: Selected Poems
    (with James Wright and John Knoepfle)
Lorca and Jiménez: Selected Poems
When Grapes Turn to Wine (Rumi)
The Lightning Should Have Fallen on Ghalib
    (with Sunil Dutta)
Kabir: Ecstatic Poems
Mirabai: Ecstatic Poems (with Jane Hirshfield)

ALSO BY LEONARD LEWISOHN

Beyond Faith and Infidelity: The Sufi Poetry and
    Teachings of Mahmud Shabistari
The Wisdom of Sufism

Edited Works
The Heritage of Sufism:
    Volume 1: The Legacy of Medieval Persian Sufism
    Volume 2: Classical Persian Sufism from Its Origins
    to Rumi
    Volume 3: Late Classical Persianate Sufism: The
    Safavid and Mughal Period (with David Morgan)
Attar and the Persian Sufi Tradition: The Art of
    Spiritual Flight (with Christopher Shackle)

The Angels Knocking on the Tavern Door

THIRTY POEMS *of* HAFEZ

Translated by
Robert Bly *and*
Leonard Lewisohn

HARPER PERENNIAL

NEW YORK • LONDON • TORONTO • SYDNEY • NEW DELHI • AUCKLAND

HARPER ●PERENNIAL

FIRST HARPER PERENNIAL EDITION PUBLISHED 2009.

Designed by Emily Cavett Taff

The Library of Congress has catalogued the hardcover edition as
follows:
Hafiz, 14th cent.
[Poems. English. Selections]
The angels knocking on the tavern door : thirty poems of Hafez /
translated by Robert Bly and Leonard Lewisohn.—1st ed.
p.   cm.
ISBN 978-0-06-113883-6
I. Bly, Robert.   II. Lewisohn, Leonard.   III. Title.
PK6465.Z31B65   2008
891'.5511—dc22   2007027894

ISBN 978-0-06-113884-3 (pbk.)

09 10 11 12 13   ID/RRD   10 9 8 7 6 5 4 3 2 1

Contents

Some Thoughts on Hafez

BY ROBERT BLY

MOST OF THE THINKING poems we admire by Wordsworth or Wallace Stevens proceed in a gentlemanly way down the page, and we all love that. But Hafez's poems move in a jagged manner. Encouraged by the ghazal form, which asks for a poem to begin again with each stanza, Hafez constantly interrupts his own flow of thought in a way unusual to us. A stanza on the glory of the countryside in spring will be followed by an aggressive attack on fundamentalists in the next stanza, and that followed by a stanza hoping for the door of mercy to be opened.

One has to be light on one's feet to read a Hafez poem all the way through. A poem of his might begin in some prehistorical time, before the creation of human beings, and that would lead directly to a description of Muhammad as a fisherman with a net or to a complaint that Hafez is wasting his life.

Hafez gives out a hundred blessings each time he lays out a poem. He tells secrets of the inner life, praises wine, and describes the gorgeous complications of certain poems written long before his.

Something in the opulence of his language reminds us of

Andrew Marvell; something in his swiftness reminds us of the young Shakespeare. Beyond these, we sense some ability to leap that many of us have never experienced before. He says:

No one has ever seen your face, and yet a thousand
Doorkeepers have arrived. You are a rose still closed,
And yet a hundred nightingales have arrived.

Hafez often teaches the poets to write about the world before this one. He praises the taverns inside Shiraz, the fields outside, the upper lips of beautiful women, the charm of wine and conversation, and the beauty of young men or young women. But always he wants us to remember

The pearl that was never inside the shell of space and time.

And we as a people are so used to being inside space and time, inside boring sermons and bad streets, that when we ask others about the pearl, we tend to inquire from "people lost at the ocean's edge," in other words, from people like us.

But he says there is someone called "the tavern master," who knows a lot. He is hinting here at the old Zoroastrian religion, which was the religion in Iran before the Muslims came. He asks:

Last night at the tavern,
When I was drunk and ruined, what glad news
Did Gabriel bring from the invisible world?

Since our natural home is Paradise, he turns to the reader and asks:

Your perch is on the lote tree in Paradise,
Oh wide-seeing hawk, what are you doing
Crouching in this mop closet of calamity?

He is not going to be overly cheerful with us:

Let the nightingale
Lover cry. Cry on. This is a place of wailing.

The English that we use in poetry now has unfortunately lost much of the moxie, fierceness, and complicated beauty that was in English at the time of Shakespeare, and so, in order to be fair to Hafez, we ought to reach for some romantic, complicated, or unusual words. But we usually fail.

We have to be clear that much has been lost in these translations. We can mourn over that, but translating them ten more times probably wouldn't do any good.

Don't allow your inward being to be hurt by what
You have or have not. Be glad, because every
Perfect thing is on its way to nonexistence.

Part I

HOW BLAME HAS BEEN HELPFUL

We are drunken ecstatics who have let our hearts
Go to the wild. We are musty scholars
Of love, and old friends of the wine cup.

People have aimed the arrow of guilt a hundred times
In our direction. With the help of our Darling's eyebrow,
Blame has been a blessing, and has opened all our work.

Oh, dark-spotted flower, you endured pain all night,
Waiting for the wine of dawn; I am that poppy
That was born with the burning spot of suffering.

If our Zoroastrian master has become disgusted
With our way of repentance, tell him, Go ahead,
Strain the wine. We are standing here with our heads down.

It is through you that our work goes on at all;
Oh, teacher of the way, please throw us a glance.
Let's be clear about it; we have fallen off the path.

Don't imagine us to be like the tulip, who is preoccupied
With its goblet shape; rather look at the dark
Spot of grief we have set on our scorched hearts.

"Hafez," you say, "what about all your intriguing colors
And ingenious fantasies?" Don't take our language seriously.
We are a clean slate on which nothing has been written.

MY CLOAK STAINED WITH WINE

Last night I walked, sleep-stained, to the door
Of the tavern. My prayer rug
And my patched cloak both were stained with wine.

A young Zoroastrian boy stepped tauntingly
From the door; "Wanderer, wake up!"
He said, "The way you walk has the stain of sleep.

"Our place is a tavern of ruin, so
Wash in clear water, so that you
Will not leave stains on this holy house.

"You are yearning for the sweet lips of boys;
But how long will you stain your spiritual
Substance with this ruby-colored wine?

"The way station of old age is one to pass
Cleanly; don't let the robe of honorable age
Be stained as it was by the rashness of youth.

"The great lovers have found their way
Into the deep ocean, and drowned
Without ever taking one stain from the sea.

"Become clean and pure; come up
Out of nature's well! How could purity ever
Be found in well water stained with mud?"

I said to the Soul of the World: "A book of roses
Has no fault. How could the season
Of spring be stained by pure wine?"

The Great One replied: "Just cut out selling your friends
These subtle ideas." "Hafez," I said,
"The grace of the teacher is often stained with rebukes."

THE NIGHT VISIT

Her hair was still tangled, her mouth still drunk
And laughing, her shoulders sweaty, the blouse
Torn open, singing love songs, her hand holding a wine cup.

Her eyes were looking for a drunken brawl,
Her mouth full of jibes. She sat down
Last night at midnight on my bed.

She put her lips close to my ear and said
In a mournful whisper these words: "What is this?
Aren't you my old lover? Are you asleep?"

The friend of wisdom who receives
This wine that steals sleep is a traitor to love
If he doesn't worship that same wine.

Oh, ascetics, go away. Stop arguing with those
Who drink the bitter stuff, because it was precisely
This gift the divine ones gave us in Pre-Eternity.

Whatever God had poured into our goblet
We drank, whether it was the wine
Of heaven or the wine of drunkenness.

The laughter of the wine, and the disheveled curls
Of the One We Love . . . How many nights of repentance—like
Hafez's—have been broken by moments like this?

THE WORLD IS NOT ALL THAT GREAT

The stuff produced in the factories of space and time
Is not all that great. Bring some wine, because
The sweet things of this world are not all that great.

Heart and soul are born for ecstatic conversation
With the Soul of Souls. That's it. If that fails,
Heart and soul are not in the end that great.

Don't become indebted to the Tuba and Sidra trees
Just to have shade in Heaven. My cypress friend,
On second glance, those trees are not all that great.

The true kingdom comes to you without any breaking
Of bones. If that weren't so, achieving the Garden
Through your own labors wouldn't be all that great.

In the five days remaining to you in this rest stop
Before you go to the grave, take it easy, give
Yourself time, because time is not all that great.

You who offer wine, we are waiting on the lip
Of the ocean of ruin. Take this moment as a gift; for the distance
Between the lip and the mouth is not all that great.

The state of my being—miserable and burned
To a crisp—is proof enough that my need
To describe my condition is not all that great.

You puritans on the cold stone floor, you are not safe
From the tricks of God's zeal: the distance between the cloister
And the Zoroastrian tavern is not, after all, that great.

The name of Hafez has been well inscribed in the books,
But in our clan of disreputables, the difference
Between profit and loss is not all that great.

A THOUSAND DOORKEEPERS

No one has ever seen your face, and yet a thousand
Doorkeepers have arrived. You are a rose still closed,
And yet a hundred nightingales have arrived.

I may be a long way from you. Oh, God,
I don't want anyone to be distant! But I know
There is possibility for a close union with you.

If I should find myself in your neighborhood one day,
There's nothing strange in that, because thousands
Of strangers constantly mill about in this town.

Is there any lover whose darling never threw
A fond look at his face? Friend, there is not enough pain
In you. With enough pain, the doctor would be here.

In this matter of love, let's not put the Sufi gathering house
In this spot and the tavern in another; in every spot of the universe
Light shines out from the face of the Friend.

There where the good work of the Muslim cloister
Is celebrated, we celebrate as well the bell
Of the monk's cell and the name of the Cross.

The cries that Hafez has made all of his life
Have not gone to waste; a strange story has emerged
Inside those cries, and a marvelous way of saying.

DO NOT SINK INTO SADNESS

Joseph the lost will return, Jacob should not
Sink into sadness; those who sit in the Grief
House will eventually sit in the Garden.

The grieving chest will find honey; do not let
The heart rot. The manic hysterical head
Will find peace; do not sink into sadness.

If the way the Milky Way revolves ignores
Your desires for one or two days, do not
Sink into sadness: All turning goes as it will.

I say to the bird: "As long as spring
Baptizes the grass, the immense scarlet blossoms
Will continue to sway over your head."

Even if the flood of materialism
Drowns everything, do not sink into
Sadness, because Noah is your captain.

Do not sink into sadness, even though the mysteries
Of the other world slip past you entirely.
There are plays within plays that you cannot see.

When you're lost in the desert, full of longing
For the Kaaba, and the Arabian thornbush
Pierces your feet, do not sink into sadness.

Although the way station you want to reach
Is dangerous and the goal distant, do not
Sink into sadness; all roads have an end.

God knows our whole spiritual state: separated
From Him and punished by rivals. Still do not
Sink into sadness. God is the one who changes conditions.

Oh, Hafez, in the darkness of poverty and in
The solitude of the night, as long as you can sing
And study the Qur'an, do not sink into sadness.

THE PEARL ON THE OCEAN FLOOR

We have turned the face of our dawn studies
Toward the drunkard's road. The grace earned from our prayers
We have turned over to the road of the Beloved.

The hot brand which we have pressed onto
Our lunatic hearts is so intense it would set fire
To the straw piles of a hundred reasonable ascetics.

The Sultan of Pre-Eternity gave us the casket of love's grief
As a gift; therefore we have turned our face
Toward this wrecked caravanserai that we call "the world."

From now on I will leave no doors in my heart open
For the love of beautiful creatures; I have placed
The signet seal of Her lips on the door of this house.

It's time to turn away from make-believe under our robes
Patched so many times. The foundation for our work
Is a tricksterish attitude that sees through all these games.

How can this wobbly old ship keep going
When in the end we have set for our soul
The task of finding the pearl on the ocean floor?

The man next door, whom I have called a parasite
Of reason and an intellectual is—thanks to God—
Like us, actually faithless and without heart.

We are content, just as Hafez is, with a phantom of you.
Oh, God, how pitifully poor our aspirations are,
And how estranged and distant, how far we are from union!

THE LOST DAUGHTER

Send out the criers, go to the marketplace of souls,
"Hear, hear, all you in the colonnade of lovers, here it is:

"For several days now, the daughter of the vine is reported lost.
Call all your friends! Whoever's near her is in danger.

"Her dress is ruby colored; her hair is done in seafoam;
She takes away reason; be alert; watch out for her!

"If you find this bitter one you can have my soul for dessert.
If she's in the Underworld, then that's the place to go.

"She's a night woman, shameless, disreputable, and red.
If you do find her, please bring her to Hafez's house."

SAY GOOD-BYE. IT WILL SOON BE OVER.

The breath of the holy musk will drift toward us
On the dawn wind once more; everything will begin to move.
The decrepit old world will be young once more.

The Judas tree with its ruddy blossoms will offer
Wine to the jasmine, and the eye of the narcissus
Will turn its loving gaze on the red peony.

The nightingale who has endured a grievous separation
Will fly now to the court of the rose,
Demanding reparations with his wild cries.

If I've left the orthodox mosque and made my way
To the tavern of ruin, don't scold me. The preachers'
Sermons are long-winded and the day is soon over.

Heart, listen to me; if you postpone the delight
Of today until tomorrow, who will guarantee
That our cash in the bank will still be here in the morning?

Keep holding the cup during the month of Shaban
Because this sun-cup will disappear from sight
Until the celebratory night at the end of Ramadan.

The rose is a precious being; its intimate conversation
Is a gift from God. It has found its way to the garden
Through one gate, and will leave through the other.

Musician, please listen! What we have here is a gathering
Of friends, so sing songs and ghazals. Why keep jabbering
About what has happened and what may happen next?

For your sake, Hafez has come into the world of existence.
As a way of saying farewell, come a step or two
Closer to him, say good-bye, for he will be very soon gone!

THE MAN WHO ACCEPTS BLAME

I'm well known throughout the whole city
For being a wild-haired lover; and I'm that man who has
Never darkened his vision by seeing evil.

Through my enthusiasm for wine, I have thrown the book
Of my good name into the water; but doing that ensures that
The handwriting in my book of grandiosity will be blurred.

Let's be faithful to what we love; let's accept blame
And keep our spirits high, because on our road, being
Hurt by the words of others is a form of infidelity.

I said to the master of the tavern: "Tell me, which is
The road of salvation?" He lifted his wine and said,
"Not talking about the faults of other people."

Learn to love the beautiful faces by noticing
The light down on the face of the Friend; nothing is sweeter
Than taking a stroll around the face that has beauty.

What is our purpose in admiring the garden
Of this world? The answer is: Let the man inside
Your eye reach out and take roses from Your face.

Let's veer toward the tavern, and turn our horses
Away from the formal church. It's incumbent not to listen
To the sermons of the man who never acts on his own words.

I have great confidence in the mercy hiding in the tips
Of your curly ringlets! If there were no evidence of grace
On the other side, what would be the point of all our effort?

Don't kiss anything except the sweetheart's lip
And the cup of wine, Hafez; friends, it's a grave mistake
To kiss the hand held out to you by a puritan.

Part II

THE WINE MADE BEFORE ADAM

When the one whom I love accepts the wine,
Then the shop of the false idols collapses.

I have dropped in a heap on the earth, crying,
In the hope that I will feel a touch of his hand.

I have fallen like a fish into deep water
In the hope that the Friend will catch me in his net.

Whoever looks into his luminous eyes cries:
"Someone is already drunk, get the police!"

How blessèd is the man who, like Hafez,
Has tasted in his heart the wine made before Adam.

CONVERSATION WITH THE TEACHER

The crude heart for years begged us for Jamshid's cup.
The heart already had it, but kept asking strangers for it.

The pearl that was never inside the shell of space and time—
We asked that from people lost at the ocean's edge.

I brought my problem last night to the tavern master
Who could see the secrets hidden in the old riddles.

I saw how happy he was, holding the wine cup in his hand,
Peering hundreds of ways into the wine-mirror.

I said, "When did God give you this world-revealing goblet?"
He said, "On the long-ago day when He raised up this blue dome!"

He added, "Our friend who made the stairs of the gallows seem
So high committed the mistake of revealing the mysteries.

"Were the grace of the Holy Spirit to visit us one more time,
Then other people, too, could perform the miracles of Jesus."

I said to him, "What is the purpose of the chainlike curls ador-
able women have?"
He said, "Hafez, you're complaining; you need these links to tie
up your own wild heart!"

GABRIEL'S NEWS

Come, come, this Pantheon of desire is set
On wobbly stones. Bring some wine,
For the joists of life are laid on the winds.

The man who can walk beneath the blue wheeling
Heavens and keep his clothes free of the dark
Of attachment—I'll agree to be the slave of his high will.

What can I tell you? Last night at the tavern,
When I was drunk and ruined, what glad news
Did Gabriel bring from the invisible world?

"Your perch is on the lote tree in Paradise,
Oh, wide-seeing hawk, what are you doing
Crouching in this mop closet of calamity?

"People on the battlements of heaven are
Blowing a whistle to bring you back.
How does it happen that you tripped the noose?

"I'll give you this advice: Please learn it
And practice it well. These few words
Were given to me by my teacher on the Path.

"Don't expect this rotten world to be faithful
To you. She has you tight by the belt. She is an old hag
Who has already slept with a thousand lovers.

"Don't let the sorrow of the world bite your soul—
Don't forget what I say. A traveler walking
The road taught me this subtlety about love:

"Be content with what you have now;
Smooth out your forehead. The door of free will
Has never been open for you or for me.

"The smile you see on the face of the rose does
Not imply promises given or kept. Let the nightingale
Lover cry. Cry on. This is a place of wailing."

You writers who write such bad poems, why
Do you envy Hafez so much? His grace of speech
That people love comes entirely from God.

ONE ROSE IS ENOUGH

One rosy face from the world's garden for us is enough,
And the shade of that one cypress in the field
Strolling along gracefully for us is enough.

I want to be far away from people whose words
And deeds don't match. Among the morose and heavy-
Hearted, a heavy glass of wine for us is enough.

Some people say that good deeds will earn them
A gated house in heaven. Being rakes and natural beggars,
A room in the tavern for us is enough.

Sit down beside the stream sometime and watch
Life flow past. That brief hint of this world
That passes by so swiftly for us is enough.

Look at the flow of money and the suffering
Of the world. If this glimpse of profit and loss
Is not enough for you, for us it is enough.

The dearest companion of all is here. What
Else is there to look for? The delight of a few words
With the soul friend for us is enough.

Don't send me away from your door, oh, God,
Even to Paradise. Your alleyway, compared
To all space and time, for us is enough.

It's inappropriate, Hafez, for you to complain
Of your gifts from Fate. Your nature is like water;
Your beautifully flowing poems for us are enough.

REAPING WHEAT

Don't worry so much about the rogues and rakes,
You high-minded puritans. You know the sins of others
Will not appear written on your foreheads anyway.

Whether I am good or bad is not exactly to the point.
Go ahead and be who you are. This world we live in
Is a farm, and each of us reaps our own wheat.

Whether we are drunk or sober, each of us is making
For the street of the Friend. The temple, the synagogue,
The church, and the mosque are all houses of love.

In my submission, I lower my head to the bricks
At the tavern door. If my critic can't understand this,
His head must have something in common with brick.

Don't make me lose hope in the grace given to us
In Pre-Eternity. What firm knowledge do you have
About what goes on behind the dark curtain?

I'm not the only one who has fallen away
From the holy cell; my father Adam himself
Let the eternal heaven slip out of his hands.

If your inner nature contains so much virtue,
That must be deeply sublime! If your basic being
Has so much goodness, it must be deeply superior!

Hafez, if it should be that your hand closes
Around a cup of wine at the moment of death,
You will go from the Magian tavern straight to heaven.

THE GREEN HEAVEN

The green cultivated fields of the firmament I did see,
And I saw the curved knife of the new moon; I remembered
The seeds I had sown, and the time of harvest.

I said, "Bad luck. My lucky star has gone down, and the sun
Has already risen." In reply, Fortune said, "Despite all this,
Do not forget the blessing laid down for you long ago."

Like Jesus, ascend on the night of your death
Straight up to heaven—so that from your lantern
A hundred rays of light will reach the sun.

Don't depend on that gift-giving star; it is
A midnight thief, for this thief has stolen the throne
Of King Kavas, and the belt worn by Kay-Kusraw.

Although your gold and ruby earrings may weigh
Down your ear a bit, listen to my advice:
The time of pleasant fairness doesn't last long.

May the evil eye be far from your beauty spot,
For in the field of beauty your mole puts forward a pawn
That moves across the board and takes both sun and moon.

Tell the heavens not to brag so much about their majesty.
The moon's gifts, compared to Love's, amounts
To one grain of wheat, and the Pleiades to two.

Hypocrisy and the fire of ascetic renunciation
Will eventually consume the harvest of religion.
Hafez, throw off your Sufi robe and go on your way.

WHAT DO WE REALLY NEED?

If a soul has already chosen solitude, why should it need
Travel? We know the street where the Friend
Lives. So why do we need the countryside?

My dear soul, by virtue of the fact that you
Have a desperate need for God, take
A moment and ask what it is we really need.

Oh, Lord of Divine Loveliness, we have been
Burned to a crisp. Come now, ask of us
What is it a destitute and beggarly person needs?

We are the lords of owning nothing. But we have
No tongue to use for requests. Is there a need
For appeal when we're already with the generous?

There is no need to go over this again. Since your thing
Precisely is spilling our blood, everything in the house
Already belongs to you. Do you need to take more?

Solomon's cup, in which all the world could be seen,
Is the bright soul of the Friend. When the Friend is with us,
What need do we have to reel off our list of demands?

The time is past that I would make myself
Indebted to a sailor; when we have found the pearl,
Do we need to keep going to the sea?

Oh, destitute lover, since the quickening kiss of the Friend
Has been granted to you in perpetuity, what need
Is there really to go on asking for good things?

Go away, you false face, I want nothing
To do with you. Lovers with true hearts
Are with us. Why should we need people like you?

Hafez, bring this to an end now. We all know
How clear your poems are. So we don't need
To quarrel with those who can't grasp poetry.

THE ANGELS AT THE TAVERN DOOR

Last night I heard angels pounding on the door
Of the tavern. They had kneaded the clay of Adam,
And they threw the clay in the shape of a wine cup.

I am a nobody, just a squatter sitting in the dust
Of the public street; and yet these sacred beings from
The Innermost Sanctuary drank some wine with me.

The heavens could not bear the weight of the Trust.
When the lots were thrown again, the Trust
Fell on man, on me, an idiot and a fool.

Let's forgive the seventy-two sects for their ridiculous
Wars and misbehaviors. Because they couldn't accept
The path of truth, they took the road of moonshine.

Thanks be to God, the Darling whom I love and I
Live in peace. Each time the playful angels in Paradise catch
Sight of us, they reach for their wineglasses and dance.

The fire is not that physical fire that makes
The candle seem to laugh. The true fire
Is the flame which consumes the treasures of the moth.

Ever since the original pen first combed the curly hair
Of speech, no one has drawn aside the veil
From the face of thought more gracefully than Hafez does.

DECIDING NOT TO GO TO INDIA

To spend even one moment grieving about this world
Is a waste of time. Let's go and sell our robes
For ordinary wine. Who says robes are better than wine?

In the crooked alleys where the wine sellers
Hang out, a prayer mat may not buy even
One glass of wine. What does that say about prayer mats?

The tavern keeper scolded me, saying I should turn
My face away from the door. What is this?
The dust on a doorsill has more value than a head?

Hidden inside the crown of a king there's always
A fear of assassination; a crown is a stylish hat,
But a head is too much to pay for it.

It seemed quite easy to put up with the ocean
And its torments to receive a profit, but I was wrong;
A hurricane is too much to pay for a hundred pearls.

It's better if you turn your face away from your
Admirers; the joy the general receives from dominating
The world is not worth the suffering of the army.

It's best to aim—as Hafez does—for contentment, and abandon
What belongs to the low world; one grain of indebtedness
To the base life weighs more than a hundred bushels of gold.

THE WIND IN SOLOMON'S HANDS

Don't expect obedience, promise keeping, or rectitude
From me; I'm drunk. I've been famous for carrying
A wine pitcher around since the First Covenant with Adam.

That very moment when I washed myself in the Spring
Of Love, that very moment I said, "God is great!"
Four times over the world, as over a corpse.

Give me some wine so I can pass on news of the mystery
Of Fate, and whose face it is with whom I have fallen
In love, and whose fragrance has made me drunk.

The withers of a mountain are actually slimmer
Than the withers of an ant. Please, you wine lovers,
Don't lose hope about the door of mercy being open.

Except for the nodding narcissus blossom—may no
Evil eye touch it—no creature has ever been
Really comfortable beneath this turquoise dome.

It's all right for my soul to be sacrificed to your mouth, because
In the Garden of Contemplation, no bud has ever
Been created by the Gardener of the World sweeter than yours.

Purely because of his love for you, Hafez became
As rich as Solomon; and from his longing for union with you,
Like Solomon, he has nothing but wind in his hands.

Part III

RECITING THE OPENING CHAPTER

How marvelous the music of that musician is
Who calls up love. The tunes he strikes up
In different modes all go to a different place.

I hope the world will never be deprived of the cries
Of lovers. When they cry out, their
Harmonies stretch us out into eternity.

Our teacher, who gobbles down the bitter stuff,
Has neither aristocracy nor gold, but he has
A sweet god of mercy who covers up our faults.

Give honor to my heart, because when it was carried
Off by the wind of passion, then this housefly in love
With sugar took on the majesty of the Huma bird.

When the King has a beggarly dervish in his neighborhood,
It's well within the scope of royal justice
If the King asks how it is with that beggar.

I brought my bloody tears to my doctor.
He said: "These symptoms all associate with love problems.
Burning and bitter medicines are indicated."

Don't allow the flirty side-glances of beauties
To teach you injustice. We know that in the religion of love
Each act returns with its own consequences.

A beautiful Christian boy who adored wine
Spoke these sweet words. He said, "Let's toast the man
Or woman in whose face we see purity and joy."

I say to King Khosrow, Hafez is sitting in your court,
And reciting the opening chapter of the Qur'an.
In return he asks a prayer from you.

BECOME A LOVER

Don't tell the mysteries of drunkenness and love
To a pedant. Let him pass away on his own,
With his ignorance and self-centeredness still inside.

If you feel weak, feeble, and powerless, well,
So does the breeze. Being sick on the Path is a hundred
Times better than a healthy mind in a healthy body.

As long as you see yourself as learned and intellectual,
You'll lodge with the idiots; moreover, if you
Can stop seeing yourself at all, you will be free.

If you are living in your dear one's castle, don't even think
About the heavens above; because if you do,
You'll drop like a stone to the filth-covered street.

Become a lover; if you don't, one day the affairs of the world
Will come to an end, and you'll never have had even
One glimpse of the purpose of the workings of space and time.

On the spiritual road, being uncooked and raw
Is a mark of unbelief; it's best to move along the path
Of fortune with nimbleness and springy knees.

In a nook safe from blame, how can we stay
Secluded when your dark eye reminds us
Always of the joy and mysteries of drunkenness?

Long ago I had a premonition of these riots
That have now occurred, when with a proud turn
Of the head you refused to sit quietly with us.

Although the thorn hurts your spirit, the rose asks pardon
For this wound; the sourness of wine is more easily tolerated
When one remembers the sweet flavor of drunkenness.

Hafez, your love is going to turn you over to the rough hand
Of the hurricane. Why did you imagine that, like a lightning
Bolt, you could free yourself from this storm?

THE DUST OF THE DOORWAY

I am not about to abandon love, nor the secret Witness,
Nor the cup of wine. I have sworn off these things
A hundred times, and I won't do it again.

I won't agree, either, that the Garden of Paradise,
The shade trees of Heaven, and the dancing of playful angels
Are as good as the ragged dust of your street.

Everything the great Teachers have to say
Amounts to a single hint. I have already
Dropped that hint once. I won't drop it again.

The only time I receive any grasp of the state
Of my own mind is when, lying flat,
I can't lift my head from the tavern floor.

The counselor spoke contemptuously to me;
He said, "Wine is forbidden, period." "I agree
With you," I said. "Also I don't listen to every jackass."

"Don't stay here," the angry shaykh said,
"And, by the way, give up love." "There's no need, brother,
For a fight here; I simply won't do that."

The probity I have is right for me. I don't go
Up in the pulpit, flirt, and throw glances
To the beautiful young women who are present.

Hafez, the arched door of the Zoroastrian master
Is a site of wealth and abundance. As for kneeling and kissing
The dust of that doorway, I will keep on doing that.

GOBBLING THE SUGAR OF DAWN SLEEP

Both human beings and spirits take their sustenance
From the existence of love. The practice of devotion
Is a good way to arrive at happiness in both worlds.

Because you aren't worthy of the side glance
Of the Darling, don't try for union. Looking directly
Into Jamshid's cup doesn't work for the blind.

But make an effort, Mr. Lordly Person, don't miss out
On your share of love. No one buys a slave if he
Hasn't a single accomplishment in grace or art.

How long will you gobble down the wine of sunrise
And the sugar of dawn sleep? Ask for forgiveness
In the middle of the night and cry when dawn comes.

Come! And with the funds provided by your beauty
Buy the kingdom from us. Don't let this deal
Slip away; you will regret it if you do.

The prayers of the people who live in the corners
Keep disaster away. Why help them
With a single glance from the corner of your eye?

Both union with you and separation from you
Confuse me. What can I do? You are not present
Nor are you utterly absent from my sight.

A thousand holy souls have been burned up
By this jealousy: in every dawn and dusk, you are
The candle that's lit in the center of a different group.

Since every bit of news I hear opens a different
Door to bewilderment, from now on I'll take
The road of drunkenness and the path of knowing nothing.

Come, come—the condition of the world as I see it
Is such that if you checked up on it,
You'd sip wine rather than your old familiar grief.

Because of the good offices of Hafez, we can
Still hope that on some moonlit night we'll
Be able to enjoy our love conversation once more.

ABOUT DESTITUTE LOVERS

Whoever has a gathered mind and a flirtatious,
Roguish darling, will find blessedness standing
Next to him, and inner wealth sitting at his right hand.

The holy court of love is a thousand times higher
Than the house of reason. Only a man who holds his soul
Lightly on his sleeve can kiss the threshold of that court.

It's a question whether your lips so sweetly closed
Have the power of Solomon's ring. But the signet stamp
Of your lips has the whole world under its imprint.

Reddish lips and the musky down on the cheek—
She may have this, and not have that, like many women.
I praise my darling, whose beauty has both this and that.

As long as you are walking on earth, recognize that
Your strength is a godsend; you know the era of impotence
Will last a long time once you are under the earth.

Do not disparage the weak and the skinny. Remember that,
You men of wealth. We know the one given the chief seat
In the Gathering is the sadhu sleeping in the street.

The prayers of the truly needy are the prayers that lift calamities
Away from body and soul. How can you receive good
From your harvest if you are ashamed to share it with the gleaners?

Dear morning wind, take this secret message of my love
To the King of Beauty, because a hundred Jamshids
And Khosrows sweep up dust from his floor.

And if the King of Beauty says, "I don't want a destitute
Lover like Hafez," just say, "Kingship
Has always had poverty as its secret partner."

THE ONE WHO REMAINS DISGRACED

When your Face became suddenly visible in the wine cup,
And it seemed as if you were the one laughing, and not
The wine, the Knower fell into a raw and giddy desire.

On the day of Pre-Eternity, your Face in its glory
Broke through from behind the veil. All of these forms
Fell into the vast mirroring sea of imagination.

All of these images and shapes that have come forth
Are actually arriving from one single luminous ray
From the cup holder's face, which has fallen into the cup.

The jealousy of love has severed the tongues of all
The Gnostics. How could it be that the mystery of His grief
Has settled down to the people walking along the street?

I did not fall away from the mosque to the tavern of ruin
By my own wish; everything that has happened to me
Took place through some agreement made in Pre-Eternity.

What can be done? For each of us who has fallen
Down into time, the situation is the same as the needle faces
Inside the compass: there is no way to keep from turning.

Whenever the Divine One waves her saber of sorrow
We'll have to dance wildly, because whomever
She kills will end up with a good situation.

The heart grabbed hold of the curl, and pulled itself
Out of the well of the chin, but once out of the well,
It fell into the dangerous snare of love and ecstasy.

A long time has passed, friend, since you saw me
Meditating in a cloister. All of my affairs now circle around
The face of the wine holder and the lip of the wineglass.

Burned up and miserable, in every breath I take,
She treats me with a different grace. Look at this beggar
Who has become worthy of receiving gifts.

The Sufis make a good show, and they know how
To play the game of glances; but among them, Hafez,
Melancholic and burned out, remains completely disgraced.

THE GUESTHOUSE WITH TWO DOORS

The red rose has broken open, and the nightingale
Is drunk. You Sufis who love each moment
Freed from time, this amounts to a call to joy.

The bedrock of our famous repentance seemed
To be tough as granite. Look, the delicate
Glass cup has split the repentance at the first blow.

Offer us wine, because in the court of God's
Magnificence, what difference is there between the Prince
And a cop, between the sober man and the drunk?

We travelers live in the guesthouse with two doors,
And we must leave. Who cares if your life goes on
Underneath a big dome or a small one?

The waiting station of pleasure and delight
Always includes suffering. In Pre-Eternity
Our souls all bound themselves to that tragedy.

Don't allow your inward being to be hurt by what
You have or have not. Be glad, because every
Perfect thing is on its way to nonexistence.

Solomon's magnificence, his horse of wind, his grasp
Of bird language—the good man got nothing
From these; all of them were blown away in the wind.

Don't veer off your own course, lifted by the wings
And feathers of glory, because the arrow that flies high up
Stays there a moment and at last eats the earth.

Now, Hafez, how can the tongue hidden in your pen
Ever give thanks enough for the way people
Pass on your poems from hand to hand?

SOME ADVICE

I followed the path of the mad libertines for years—
Long enough, until I was able, with the consent
Of intelligence, to put my greediness into prison.

I didn't find the way to the nest of the great bird
Of the far mountain by myself. I made
The trip with the help of the bird of Solomon.

Seek satisfaction in what comes contrary
To your habit. I found interior concentration
At last in your disheveled head of hair.

Bring a cooling shade over my interior burning—
You are a hidden treasure—because it is out of the melancholy
Of desire for you that I have wrecked this house.

I repented and swore that I would never kiss
The salty lip of the cup bearer again; but now I am biting
My own lip, and I wonder why I ever listened to an idiot.

Being a model of modesty or drunkenness
Is not up to us. Whatever the Master
Of Pre-Eternity told me to do, I did.

Because of the grace of Pre-Eternity, I have a longing
For the Garden of Paradise, even though I spent
Long years as a doorkeeper in the tavern.

Here at the door of old age, the fact that the companionship
Of Joseph has graced me is a reward for my patience
When living like Jacob in his house of sorrow.

No reciter of scripture who stands in the mihrab
Of the Firmament has ever enjoyed such delight
As I have received from the wealth of the Qur'an.

A GLASS OF WINE

In this age, the only companions we have
Who are free of faults are a glass
Of clear wine and a book of love poems.

Go by yourself, for the gates of righteousness
Are narrow; take hold of the wine cup,
For nothing can equal the dearness of life.

Others beside me are fed up with this world of idleness
And useless brain labor. The weakness of academics comes
From never carrying an idea onward into days and nights.

To the eye of the spiritual intellect, this hallway
Of life, this corridor of noise, this world
And all its affairs are flat and without substance.

My heart was full of hope that it could achieve
Union with your Face; but death is a thief
Who steals all desires and keeps us from union.

Reach for her forehead and lift one of those strands
Of hair; then forget about whether Saturn
Or Venus is responsible for your luck.

A passionate note was put into Hafez on the day of creation.
In no cycle of history will you ever find him sober.
Hafez has always been drunk on the wine of Pre-Eternity.

ON THE WAY TO THE GARDEN

The Garden is breathing out the air of Paradise
Today. I can sense myself, and this lively wine,
And this friend whose nature approaches the divine.

It's all right if the beggar claims to be a king
Today. His tent is a shadow thrown by a cloud;
His banqueting hall is a newly sown field.

Paradise is here in the simple tale that the May
Meadow tells; the wise person lets the future
And its profits go, and accepts the cash now.

Please don't imagine that your enemy will ever
Be faithful to you. The candle the hermit lights
Will always flutter out in the worldly church.

Make your soul strong then by letting it drink
The secret wine. This rotten world has its own
Plans to press our dust into bricks.

My life is a black book. But don't rebuke a drinker
Like me too much. No human being can ever read
The words written on his own forehead.

When Hafez's coffin comes by, it'll be all right
To follow behind. Although he is
A captive of sin, he is on his way to the Garden.

Hafez and His Genius

BY LEONARD LEWISOHN

HAFEZ WAS BORN IN either 715/1315 or 717/1317, and spent all his life in the city of Shiraz in southwestern Persia, rarely leaving its gates, and died there in 791/1389. The poetry of Hafez and the city of Shiraz are as inseparable from each other as are Dante and the city of Florence. Long before Hafez's birth, Shiraz was known as the House of Knowledge, having nurtured scores of geniuses in the fields of science, mysticism, and belles lettres, including the ascetic master Ibn Khafif (who died in 982), the "Master of Paradoxes" Shaykh Ruzbihan Baqli (who died in 1210), and the sweetest of all Persian lyrical poets, Sa'di (who died around 1292). Shiraz, the "City of Saints and Poets," was renowned for its men of learning, for its princely patronage of the arts and sciences, and for the thousands of scholars, scientists, and philosophers who taught in its colleges.[1] In addition to the scholarly gnostics, elegant ascetics, and Sufi saints who made Shiraz a holy city, it also contained in its walls spacious gardens, pleasances and parks, promenades and houses of pleasure, brothels and taverns, all of which Hafez celebrated in a number of ghazals.

Some of the greatest Persian Sufi poets of the fourteenth

century flourished contemporaneously with Hafez, including 'Imad al-Din Faqih Kirmani (d. 1371), Shah Ni'matullah Wali (d. 1431), and Kamal Khujandi (d. 1400), the first two living in Kirman and the latter in Tabriz. Hafez was not on friendly terms with any of these poets, although he conducted lively poetic exchanges with all of them. Another important contemporary master lyrical poet who lived in Tabriz during this period was Salman Savaji (d. 778/1376), whose ghazals sometimes parallel those of Hafez so closely that it is clear they imitated and followed each other's poetry.

'Ubayd-i Zakani (d. 1371), one of the greatest satirical and ribald poets in Persian literature, who also wrote some wonderful erotic and bacchanalian ghazals in the style of Sa'di, moved in the same princely court circles in Shiraz that were frequented by Hafez. In his poetic parodies on the hypocrisy of Muslim clerics, charlatan Sufis, and ascetics, Hafez followed 'Ubayd's acerbic, sarcastic style. One of the most celebrated major poets of the city, whom Hafez admired and who reciprocated his admiration, was Khwaju Kirmani (who died sometime after 1352). Hafez's pursuit of the *malamati* tradition of Sufi cynicism—the courting of notoriety by calling down blame upon oneself—was anticipated clearly in Khwaju's ghazals, whose poetic style and views Hafez apparently followed closely.

Despite all the many other poets of that time, Hafez today remains *the* prime Persian poet of the fourteenth century. In fact, among all the city's sons, with the possible exception of Sa'di, he is the most celebrated; indeed he is generally considered the most eminent and most renowned of all the poets of Persia. Although it would not be until a century after his death that the poetry of Hafez was assembled and collated in the *Divan* (collected poems) form known to us today, his poems were internationally celebrated during his own lifetime, being perused and collected by lovers of poetry, not only in Persia proper but in Ottoman Turkey and India.

For several hundred years after his death, taste for his poetry was cultivated more in India and in the Ottoman world than in Persia proper. Serious scholarly interest in Hafez resurfaced in Iran less than a century ago; today myriads of printed editions of his *Divan* can be found in bookshops in Tehran, Isfahan, Shiraz, and Tabriz. Several good critical editions have appeared. Two of the best are the one compiled by Parviz Natil Khanlari, containing 486 ghazals, and that of Muhammad Qazwini and Qasim Ghani, containing some 495 ghazals. In our translation, we have relied largely on Khanlari's edition, which, despite certain shortcomings, remains in my opinion the best critical edition in print.

It is no exaggeration to say that Hafez continues to be far and away the most popular poet in Iran today. Some households in Iran can be found without a Qur'an on their bookshelves, but everyone's library contains at least one copy of Hafez's *Divan*. In the Academy, Hafez's poetry stands at the summit of the Persian literary canon of lyrical poetry, and today constitutes a virtually separate subfield of Persian literary criticism called "Hafezology." Postgraduate students in Iranian universities often spend a full year just studying Hafez under professors specially trained in exegesis of his verse. In Persian, the bibliography of books, monographs, learned articles, and commentaries on Hafez's life and verse is vast and growing every year.

HAFEZ'S THEOLOGY OF SIN

Hafez's attitude toward religion is marked by a hatred
of hypocrisy.[2] He held that hypocrisy (*ru'y u riya*), which in
Persian implies a faking of religious faith, was a far worse
evil and a graver sin than the consumption of intoxicating
beverages. Consequently, he held the simulation of abstemi-
ousness on the part of zealous Muslim prohibitionists to be
worse than drinking alcohol.

> Don't kiss anything except the sweetheart's lip
> And the cup of wine, Hafez; friends, it's a grave mistake
> To kiss the hand held out to you by a puritan.

He expresses revulsion for the ascetic abstinence (*zuhd*)
and piety (*taqwa*) of the ascetics, preferring the infamy of
the honest drunkard to the false facade of those ungracious
mullahs, who, recking not their own rede, to paraphrase
Shakespeare, pretend that the primrose path of dalliance
they tread is the steep and thorny path to heaven. In verse
after verse, he takes refuge from their pedantic self-righ-
teousness in the sweet unreason of love. He emphasizes that
Muslim religiosity is very dangerous when separated from
Eros. Hafez thus compares the Shari'a-oriented legalism of
the Muslim pharisees and ascetics to a fire that shall con-
sume all faith:

> Hypocrisy and the fire of ascetic renunciation
> Will eventually consume the harvest of religion.
> Hafez, throw off your Sufi robe and go on your way.

One of the most puzzling, even outrageous, ideas expounded by Hafez is his defense of sin. It is important to sin to know God.[3] In fact, Hafez declares that salvation is impossible without sin.[4] According to Sufi doctrine, sin is to wisdom as fuel is to fire.[5] Hafez, in a poem modeled after (written in the same rhyme and meter) the Isma'ili poet Nizari Quhistani (d. 1321), thus wrote:

My life is a black book. But don't rebuke a drinker
Like me too much. No human being can ever read
The words written on his own forehead.

When Hafez's coffin comes by, it'll be all right
To follow behind. Although he is
A captive of sin, he is on his way to the Garden.

Blake, too, cursed and condemned orthodox Christianity as being "Satan's Synagogue" in his poem "The Everlasting Gospel":

The Vision of Christ that thou dost see
Is my Vision's Greatest Enemy . . .

HAFEZ'S LIFE, TIMES, AND WAY OF BLAME

Of Hafez's early life—his birth, his schooling—we can be sure of almost nothing.[6] Everyone agrees, and his poems attest, that he knew the Qur'an by heart. It is clear that he had received an excellent theological education. We have nothing definitive about Hafez's relations with women or his marriage.

A number of Hafez's most bitter attacks on orthodoxy were composed during the five-year reign (1353–1357) of Mubariz al-Din Muzaffar; he ruled Shiraz as a kind of police state and was "orthodox, harsh, and not inclined to spare human life."[7]

> After he conquered the province of Fars, he [Mubariz al-Din] . . . gave encouragement to the puritan ascetics, the jurisprudents, and the severe *Shari'a*-oriented clerics.[8]

The historian Abd al-Husayn Zarrinkub explains the political climate at that time:

> During Mubariz al-Din's reign of terror, "dangerous books" as our government today labels them, or "useless texts" (*kutub mahrumat al-intifa'*) as they were then known, were collected and their pages were washed clean. It is even said that once he found some irreligious sentiments, shortcomings of orthodox faith and tendencies towards sin in certain poems by Sa'di that he'd read and demanded that his mausoleum be burnt down. Fortunately his own son Shah Shuja' intervened and persuaded him to change his mind, assuring him that he was personally confident of Sa'di's penitent and pious nature. . . . By Mubariz al-Din's order, all the taverns were closed down, their casks of wine emptied in the streets, and the town's dens of vice

(*kharabat*) boarded up. When the doors of the taverns are shut, what other shop will be left open except that of religious hypocrisy? This "born-again" king, who had just opened his own shop with these wares of religious hypocrisy, was nicknamed the "policeman" by the rogues of the city. This "policeman" was notorious for his excessively cruel and ruthless nature, where it was said that he would sit in his chamber reciting the Qur'an, and then would have criminals summoned before him, rise from his place and kill them with his own hands, before resuming his recitation.[9]

In this oppressive climate, it is easy to see how Hafez could prefer the Sufi "inspired libertine" (*rind*) over the conventional hero, and declare:

I followed the path of the mad libertines for years—
Long enough, until I was able with the consent
Of intelligence to put my greediness into prison.

To take in what Hafez is saying here, it's important to grasp the nature of the three outrageous beings, the *qalandar*, the *rind*, and the *malamati*.

The *qalandar* is the Islamic counterpart of the Hindu *saddhu*, a holy wandering vagabond (*faqir*) who attired himself in outlandish garb, and often shaved all facial hair save the moustache, and traveled from town to town occupied in devotional practices in order to mortify his soul and disengage himself from worldly concerns. All Sufi poets and writers used the symbol of the *qalandar* to signify someone liberated from the bonds of socio-cultural convention, and it is with this connotation that this figure appeared as a popular poetic topos in the poems of Sana'i, 'Attar, and Rumi, and in the hagiography and poetry of 'Iraqi. Hafez celebrates the figure of the wandering *qalandar* throughout his verse as well.

The second tradition of "beyond the law" people is called the inspired libertine (*rind*).[10] The literary source of Hafez's doctrine of the *rind* can be traced back to the sophisticated literary tradition of poetry written in praise of the spiritual vagabonds. Although the term *rind* occurs frequently in the early Persian Sufi poets, especially in 'Attar (d. 1221), this term took on a central role only in Hafez's poetry, who made it his key concept.

The *rind* represents Hafez's most important contribution to the phenomenology of religious psychology. The *rind*'s ethic is paradoxical: he is a righteous sinner, a blessed reprobate, a pious rake, a holy renegade from faith, a loose liver whose sophisticated and refined moral values make the faith of fundamentalist puritan ascetics look trite and vulgar. At the same time he is one whose pursuit of love, adoration of beauty, and worship of wine embrace the whole spiritual universe of Persian Sufism.

The libertine is not only "inspired" in his love affairs, but his very world is spiritual—*is* inspiration. Pervert, lout, rogue, beggar, pauper, drunk . . .[11] all these epithets need to be considered in the context of Hafez's subversion of *this base world*. These terms satirize attachment to materiality, being the titles and the epithets that the poet proudly wears at war with the gilded honor and empty reputation of the exoteric realm. Hafez's belittling of the ascetic's mantle and the Sufi's tattered robe (*khirqa*), his sacrilegious oblation of wine over his own prayer carpet (*sajjada*), his breaking of the thread of his rosary (*sabha*) . . . all are an indictment of spiritual materialism, formalist piety, which is accompanied by sanctimony and hypocrisy.

The *rind* rejects the religious formalists' "right way" to live. Whether it was masquerading as religious piety, which is at heart starkly egocentric, or parading social rank and status within the garb of the dervish's "spiritual poverty" (*faqr*), Hafez understood that the material world's vulgar concerns pervaded the mosque as much as *khanaqah*, infecting the ascetic's piety as much as the Sufi's. The *rind* was often highly educated, but he refused any official position. It was his job to reject propriety and right living. He stood for wrong living. He was a libertine, but learned. He preferred Eros to propriety. Hafez embodied the *rind*.

The third tradition among people out of the mainstream from which Hafez drew inspiration was the *malamati* mystical way. The *malamati* tradition was developed in Nishapur during the eleventh century, and later became enormously popular. Followers of the *malamati* tradition later developed into separate *qalandari* Sufi orders, which, under the leadership of Jamal al-Din Sawi (d. circa 1232), became scattered all over Egypt, Libya, Turkey, Persia, and India.[12]

Both the early *malamati* mystics and the later *qalandar* wanderers were radical spiritual nonconformists. The *malamati* mystic does one thing more: he incurs blame from the community by his words or by the way he lives. His spiritual task is to take roads for which others will blame him. Hafez thus submits himself to public censure and blame, by

75

exhibiting shamelessness, outrageous behavior, perversity, and blasphemy without fearing the accusations and slander of fundamentalists. Khurramshahi mentions ten different *malamati* doctrines espoused by Hafez.[13]

Although *malamati* conceptions are generally alien to Western philosophical ethics (excluding perhaps the early Greek Cynics), it is interesting that the best summary of the underlying ideals of *malamati* spirituality by any Western writer (as far as I know) comes from the pen of Ralph Waldo Emerson, who was largely responsible for popularizing—and partially, for translating—Hafez (his favorite Oriental poet[14]) in the United States in the nineteenth century. The following quotation comes from his essay on "Compensation":

> The wise man throws himself on the side of his assailants. It is more in his interest than it is in theirs to find his weak point. The wound cicatrizes and falls off from him like a dead skin, and when they would triumph, lo! he has passed on invulnerable. Blame is safer than praise. I hate to be defended in a newspaper. As long as all that is said is said against me, I feel a certain assurance of success. But as soon as honeyed words of praise are spoken to me, I feel as one that lies unprotected before his enemies. In general, every evil to which we do not succumb is a benefactor.[15]

Considered in the light of the rich historical background and sophisticated mystical doctrines carried by the lives and words of the *qalandar*, *rind*, and *malamati* traditions, many of Hafez's images no longer appear as mere colorful

metaphors, but actually convey quite precise spiritual sig-
nificances:

> People have aimed the arrow of guilt a hundred times
> In our direction. With the help of our Darling's eyebrow,
> Blame has been a blessing, and has opened all our work.

Out of the hundreds of verses by Hafez celebrating the
malamati's road, I'll set down three stanzas from a famous
ghazal that flaunt his bacchanalian ethics and attack Muslim
fundamentalists:

> I'm notorious throughout the whole city
> As a wild-haired lover; and I'm that man who has
> Never darkened his vision by seeing evil.

> Through my enthusiasm for wine, I have thrown the book
> Of my good name into the water; but doing that ensures that
> The handwriting in my book of grandiosity will be blurred.

> Let's be faithful to what we love; let's accept reproach
> And keep our spirits high, because on our road, being easily
> Hurt by the words of others is a form of infidelity.

In the teachings of Ahmad Ghazali (who died in
1126), to which many of Hafez's doctrines are traceable,
the human spirit can abandon the temporal realm only
if and when one is subjected to public blame and abuse.
The central mystical concept here again is *malamat*: that
the lover become the butt of abuse and so be forced to
endure public blame. One way the soul can free itself
from spiritual fraudsters is through the experience of be-
ing attacked constantly by the pharisaical puritans and

77

zealots who generally command the temples, synagogues, and mosques.

Blame has a very positive effect on the spirit "because there is safety in derision," as Yeats understood. Both men say that the spirit can never sever its ties with this lower realm and approach the Beloved unless it endures blame. Blame gradually strips the lover of his egocentric selfhood and forces him to abandon all secular support; blame turns the lover away from the world first and then from himself. Indeed, without blame, no love affair ever truly begins or ends.

Mubariz al-Din, the "policeman," was finally blinded and then blessedly deposed by his own son Shah Shuja'; the son then reigned for twenty-five years (1359–1384), and many of Hafez's greatest erotic and joyful poems were composed during those years. The son himself became a poet of considerable talents, whom Hafez celebrated in several panegyrical poems, and one of his ghazals even begins: "At dawn, I heard a supernatural voice that conveyed good news to me: 'It's the Age of Shuja'—drink wine and have no fear.'"

Scholars maintain that sixty percent of all the references Hafez made to Persian princes and patrons were to Shah Shuja'. In many senses Hafez's *Divan* is as intimately tied to the fame and fortunes of Shah Shuja''s court as was *The Faerie Queene* of Spenser with Queen Elizabeth's. Hafez survived Shah Shuja' by only half a decade, and today if anyone remembers that king it is mainly because Hafez was a part of his court.

AGAINST THE PURITANS AND PHARISEES
OF ISLAM: HAFEZ'S ANTICLERICALISM

In Hafez's *Divan* there are a number of stock charac-
ters—the Preacher (*wa'iz*), Shaykh, Judge (*qadi*), and the
Lawyer or Jurist (*faqih*)—all of whom receive his contempt.
Basically, they all belong to the exoteric Muslim clergy. His
greatest enemy, the nightmare obsession of the whole *Divan*,
is the Ascetic (*zahid*). He represents the Muslim pharisee
par excellence. For several centuries in England and New
England, this sort of man was called the "Puritan" or the
"Formalist." The newspapers today refer to him as a "reli-
gious fundamentalist."[16]

This sort of Islamic puritan, sometimes called "counsel-
or" or "shaykh" in Hafez's poetry, appears in Elizabethan
England in the form of Angelo, the pharisaic deputy of the
law in Shakespeare's *Measure for Measure*. Hafez pours
ridicule on such people:

> The counselor spoke contemptuously to me;
> He said: "Wine is forbidden, period." "I agree
> With you," I said. "Also I don't listen to every jackass."

> "Don't stay here," the angry shaykh said,
> "And, by the way, give up love." "There's no need, brother
> For a fight here; I simply won't do that."

Although the ascetic claims to be devoted to reason, in
Hafez he is just a fool, like Malvolio in *Twelfth Night*. Hafez
says:

Don't kiss anything except the sweetheart's lip
And the cup of wine, Hafez; friends, it's a grave mistake
To kiss the hand held out to you by a puritan.

Elsewhere he says:

The hot brand which we have pressed onto
Our lunatic hearts is so intense it would set fire
To the straw piles of a hundred reasonable ascetics.

The ascetic is a heretic to the religion of love:

Oh, ascetics, go away. Stop arguing with those
Who drink the bitter stuff, because it was precisely
This gift the divine ones gave us in Pre-Eternity.

Here the ascetic's piety is pure sanctimony, empty of any
real religion. Hafez says to such puritans:

Don't worry so much about the rogues and rakes,
You high-minded puritans. You know the sins of others
Will not appear written on your foreheads anyway.

The most celebrated stanza Hafez wrote attacking the
ascetic's obsession with exposing the faults of others—un-
willing to cast the beam out of his own eye but ready to see
the mote in his brother's[17]—is this:

I said to the master of the tavern: "Tell me, which is
The road of salvation?" He lifted his wine and said,
"Not talking about the faults of other people."[18]

Hafez's censure of fault-finding is exactly in accordance

with the tenets of the Persian *futuwwat* tradition, where this moral vice is repeatedly condemned.[19] We also notice the many verses of Rumi's *Mathnawi* that attack the obsession with the vices of one's neighbor (*'ayb-ju'i*).[20] His idea is akin to Blake's view:

> Mutual forgiveness of each vice
> Such are the Gates of Paradise.

Hafez emphasizes the forgiveness:

> Whether I am good or bad is not exactly to the point.
> Go ahead and be who you are. This world we live in
> Is a farm, and each of us reaps our own wheat.

> Whether we are drunk or sober, each of us is making
> For the street of the Friend. The temple, the synagogue,
> The church, and the mosque are all houses of love.

ONE WAY OF TRANSLATING HAFEZ

This translation began a decade and a half ago when Robert Bly and I decided to attempt some translations of Hafez. We resolved to set aside some days or weeks each year to meet and work on nothing but the translation. We have been working now for fourteen years on these thirty ghazals.

For decades, the symbols and language of Sufism had been familiar territory to both of us. My first job was to prepare a literal, fully annotated translation of each ghazal for use as a crib. I consulted twenty or so Persian commentaries and glossaries on the *Divan* of Hafez, as well as countless dictionaries of Sufi terminology and various literary studies concentrating on his key images and ideas. Iranian scholarship of this century and the last was indispensable in identifying the literary, mystical, metaphysical, and historical contexts of the poetry. The first stage of our translation involved word-by-word translation as well as an annotated commentary I made on each poem.

The work at the start involved a kind of mapmaking: investigating the various layers of historical, cultural, and spiritual meaning hidden inside each poem. Today very few Persians, and almost no Westerners, have a grasp of the thought underlying Hafez's outrageous, romantic, and erotic imagery. Although a huge amount of historical information about his life and a large number of critical editions and studies of his poetry have appeared in print, Persian-speakers of past generations actually understood Hafez better than the people of today. This is because, as Nasru'llah Purjavadi points out:

> The literati of past generations versed in Persian
> literature lived in the same traditional world as Hafez,
> shared his faith, and understood his mysteries as rev-
> elations of the *'alam-i ma'na*, the World of Ideas.
> Their appreciation of Hafez was through the interior
> knowledge of the heart. Well acquainted with the
> World of the Spirit themselves, they understood exactly
> why indeed he is the "Tongue of the Unseen" (*lisan
> al-ghayb*). . . . Today we seek to understand Hafez

conceptually, by way of sorting out the poet's mental constructs and ideas, having forgotten the fact that the source of inspiration of true poetry hails from a realm beyond such concepts and constructs. Having lowered and degraded the spiritual symbolism of poetry down to the level of purely mental concepts, our modern appreciation of these concepts is merely conceptual and empirical, instead of spiritual and presential.

After the scholarship, we continued by turning each stanza into clear prose. That could be called the second stage. The third stage, which includes bringing the moods, sound, and rhythms of Persian into a language utterly alien to the original, proved to be even more difficult than we had expected. When each ghazal, as heavily laden with bales of references as a camel is with cargo, entered the room, several days of arguments and talk were often consumed in the translation of a single poem.

Often the investigation of the ghazal's difficult mystical theology led to revelation of the deeper spiritual structure of the verse, which now merited our careful consideration. In the following ghazal, for example, the first three lines address the theological debate in medieval Islam about whether it is possible to perceive God in *this world*. The first stanza reads:

No one has ever seen your face, and yet a thousand
Doorkeepers have arrived. You are a rose still closed,
And yet a hundred nightingales have arrived.

Khatmi Lahuri wrote a commentary on Hafez's *Divan* in India circa 1026 A.H./1617. Khurramshahi declares it to be "the clearest, best and most revealing of all ancient and modern commentaries in solving the difficulties in Hafez's poetry."[21] That work has been an indispensable source of reference for us during this translation. Here's what he says about the stanza just quoted:

> The second hemistich of this verse is related to the
> first hemistich through the rhetorical device of repeti-
> tive "folding and unfolding" (*laff u nashr*), so that for
> example, [he states] "your true-divine face and visage
> has not been seen by anyone *in this world*, and yet
> there are a thousand lovers eagerly yearning for you."
> This situation is analogous to saying that your existence
> resembles an unopened rosebud that is being courted
> by a thousand nightingales. This is opposed to the cus-
> tomary practice of the nightingale that usually only falls
> in love with the rose once it opens up and blossoms and
> diffuses its fragrance abroad.[22]

From Lahuri's lengthy commentary on this ghazal (only a tiny snippet from which was just cited), we deduce that Hafez is expressing the notion that God (= the rose) in this world remains hidden behind the veils of majesty and glory (= the thousand doorkeepers) and so is forever invisible to the optical sight and aural apprehension of man. Yet, though He cannot be seen, He still has a thousand lovers who love and yearn for Him with all their heart and soul.

The arcane mystical theology and literary referenc-es underlying the key technical terms of every line of this ghazal—as well as every other ghazal in this collection—were subjected to this sort of treatment. After we have examined the scholarship around a given ghazal, one of us would compose several versions of a given line, which would be read off to the other. Lengthy discussions would inevitably ensue. Several hours later, one, or a combination of several, of these lines would be chosen as the final translation; in some cases, if necessary, an entirely new version might be prepared.

Each of the drafts of a ghazal was then reworked over the course of several years on the basis of new research and commentaries. In sum, wherever we have taken liberties in this translation with Hafez's literal meaning, these have always been informed liberties that took into account the meaning of the verse, never the license of idle speculation. After fifteen years of work, we feel confident that these thirty ghazals have some merit.

Robert Bly has brought to this translation of Hafez not only his many years of experience in the translation of European and Latin American poets such as Jimenez, Lorca, Neruda, Machado, Trakl, Rilke, and Gunnar Ekelöf, but also his long familiarity with the translation of Oriental poets steeped in Sufism or Sufi-influenced mysticism such as Rumi, Kabir, Mirabai, and Ghalib. It was a privilege to work at his side and observe how, by dint of his fierce fidelity to preserving expressive idiomatic meaning in English verse, Hafez's ghazals have acquired a modern American style without losing their native Persian luster or elegance.

These traditions mentioned above—of the *qalandar*, or the wanderer who has given up house and home; the *rind*, or genius bad-man; and the *malamati*, who accepts blame from the community—are all three parts of a literary tradition of which in the English or American tradition we know virtually nothing. Hafez by contrast is master par excellence of symbolic language, having brought it to a degree of subtlety never again to be attained.

> What the Great Teachers have to say
> Amounts to a single hint. I have already
> Dropped that hint once. I won't drop it again.

Having done the work as well as we could, we still feel that there are enormous deficiencies in our translations, sometimes amounting to a loss of flavor, or an absence of surprise, or the imprecise evocation of a verse's deeper meanings, as well as the sacrifice of the original music. Whatever flaws may exist, we hope these versions make clear our admiration for his genius.

Notes on "Hafez and His Genius"

1. See A. J. Arberry, *Shiraz: Persian City of Saints and Poets*, (Norman, Okla.: University of Oklahoma Press, 1960); and John Limbert, *Shiraz in the Age of Hafez* (Seattle: University of Washington Press, 2004).

2. As Khurramshahi observes: "Hafez had only one sole motivation in haranguing and assailing the Preacher, Ascetic, Sufi and Policeman throughout his *Divan*. That was his struggle against hypocrisy, for these figures were high representatives of the pharisaical sanctimony and cant which typified his age." (HN, II, p. 819).

3. Yahya ibn Mu'adh Razi (d. 871) in this context declared: "The contrition of sinners is far better than the pompous pretensions and display of piety put on by sanctimonious worshippers." Ansari, *Tabaqat al-sufiyya*, pp. 7, 321; cited by Khurramshahi, HN, I, p. v. One of the followers of Abu Sa'id ibn Abi'l-Khayr (d. 440/1048) asked him: "Does a devoted worshipper of God cease to be a devotee when he sins?" "If he is a devotee, no," answered the master. "The sinning of our father Adam, peace be upon him, did not cause him to lose his rank as God's devotee or cease to be God's devotee. So be a devotee of Him, and go wherever you like. Sin accompanied

by contrition is certainly better than devotional worship with pride [as can be seen from the fact that] Adam exhibited contrition [and was saved], whereas Iblis acted with pride [and was damned]." Ibn Munawwar, *Asrar at-tawhid*, ed. Shafi'i-Kadkani, pp. 302–3; cited by Khurramshahi, *ibid.*

4. On which, see Khurramshahi, "Mayl-i Hafez bih gunah" ("Hafez's Penchant for Sin") in his *Dhihn u zaban-i Hafez* (Tehran: Intisharat-i Nahid 1379 A.H./2000), pp. 61–92.

5. Many *hadiths* of the Prophet taught sin to be the polar counterpart of virtue. One such saying states: "If you did not sin, God would have to create another company of sinners to sin that He might forgive them."

6. Khurramshahi, "ii. Hafez's Life and Times," in *Encyclopædia Iranica*, XI, p. 465.

7. Annemarie Schimmel, "Hafez and His Contemporaries," in Peter Jackson and L. Lockhart (eds.), *The Cambridge History of Iran*, vol. 6 (Cambridge: Cambridge University Press, 1986), VI, p. 934.

8. Ghani, BAA, I, p. 214.

9. *Az kucha-i rindan: dar-bara-i zindagi va andisha-i Hafez* (Tehran: Intisharat-i Amir Kabir 2536/1977), p. 51.

10. The translation of *rind* as "inspired libertine" adopted here was first pioneered by Daryoush Shayegan, "The Visionary Topography of Hafez," translated by Peter Russell, *Temenos: A Review Devoted to the Arts of the Imagination*

VI (1985), pp. 207–32; the essay later featured as the introduction to Elizabeth Grey, *The Green Sea of Heaven: Fifty Ghazals from the Dívàn of Hafez* (Ashland, Ore.: White Cloud Press, 1995).

11. Referring to some of the key terms in Hafez's *malamati* lexicon: *fasiq, awbash, rind, gida, muflis, mast.* For further study see F. Lewis, "Hafez, VIII. Hafez and *Rendi*," in *Encyclopædia Iranica*, XI, pp. 487–89.

12. T. Yazizi, "Kalandariyya," EI2, IV, p. 473; on Savi and the *qalandar*s, see Ahmet Karamustafa, *God's Unruly Friends: Dervish Groups in the Islamic Later Middle Period* (Salt Lake City: University of Utah Press 1994), pp. 40–44.

13. HN, II, pp. 1090–97.

14. On which, see John Yohannan, "The Persian Poet Hafez in England and America," Columbia University Ph.D. Dissertation (1939), pp. 120–59.

15. In *Ralph Waldo Emerson: Essays and Lectures* (New York: Library of America, 1983), p. 298.

16. Using the terms "puritan" and "fundamentalist" here is clearly unsatisfactory; my aim is only to offer a handy English idiomatic equivalence to expressions such as *zahid-i zahir-parast*, etc., that fill the *Divan*; these terms are not meant to reflect any particular historical denomination in any religion, past or present, nor do I wish to efface the full splay and delicate nuances of centuries of Muslim religious and literary historical usage of terms such as *zahid, faqih*, etc., by means

of these terminological generalizations. Needless to say, the lives and writings of many members of the historical "Puritan" movement, such as John Milton (1608–1674) and John Bunyan (1628–1688), often even give voice to their staunch opposition to the fulminations of religious zealots, occasionally after the manner of Hafez.

17. Matthew 7:3.

18. *Divan*, ed. Khanlari, ghazal 385: 4. Commenting on this verse, Lahuri (SIH, IV, p. 2563) relates an interesting tale from a certain "Treatise on the Benefits of Belief" *(Risala-yi Fawa'id al-'aqa'id)* about the ascension of the Prophet. "Having returned from the Divine Presence, the Prophet found himself standing in the midst of Paradise. He was given a robe of honour to put on. He thought to himself, 'How nice it would be if the members of my community might also receive some benefit from this robe as well.' Gabriel at that moment appeared and said, 'Indeed, the members of your community will benefit from this robe of honour but on one condition.' Upon return to his terrestrial abode, the Prophet summoned his elect Companions and related other particulars of his spiritual journey, before concluding with the above account. He commented, 'Now, I wonder if there is any among you who can fulfill that condition so I may give him this robe?' 'Umar, Uthman and Abu Bakr each rose and offered their own views about the meaning of Gabriel's binding condition, but the Prophet bade them each be seated. Finally when it came the turn of 'Ali, the Prophet asked, 'So 'Ali, to fulfill this condition, what would you do?' 'Ali replied, 'I would reveal the upright virtues *(rast)* of God's devotees and conceal their faults.' 'That, indeed, is the condition!' the Prophet said,

bestowing upon 'Ali that robe of honour *(khirqa)*, which has been passed down thenceforth to Sufi masters down to the present day. Indeed, to be a dervish totally means to conceal the faults of others."

19. See Leonard Lewisohn, "The Metaphysics of Justice and the Ethics of Mercy in the Thought of 'Ali ibn Abi Talib," in A. Lakhani (ed.), *The Sacred Foundations of Justice in Islam* (Vancouver, B.C.: Sacred Web, 2006), pp. 108–46, in which the origins of this attitude of turning a blind eye to faults I have traced back to the Persian Sufi chivalric tradition.

20. See *The Mathnawí of Jalálu'ddín Rúmí*, tr./ed. R. A. Nicholson, (London: E.J.W. Gibb Memorial Trust 1924–1940; Gibb Memorial Series N.S.), I: 1394–1402; II: 3027–45; III: 881–85; IV: 367–68.

21. SIH, introduction, p. iv.

22. SIH, I, pp. 409–10.

Abbreviations to Reference Works on Hafez's Poetry

BAA   Ghani, Qasim. *Bahth dar athar u afkar u ahwal-i Hafez*, 2 vols., vol. 1, *Tarikh-i 'asr-i Hafez ya tarikh-i fars va madafat va iyalat-i mujavarih dar qarn-i hashtum*. Tehran: Intisharat-i Zawwar 1383 A.H./2004.

DH   Isti'lami, Muhammad. *Dars-i Hafez: Naqd u sharh-i ghazalha-yi Khwaja Shams al-Din Muhammad Hafez*, 2 vols. Tehran: Intisharat-i Sukhan 1382 A.H./2003.

FAH   Bukhara'i, Ahmad 'Ali Raja'i. *Farhang-i ash'ar-i Hafiz* (*Glossary of Hafez's Verse*). Tehran: Intisharat-i 'Ilmi, 2nd ed. Tehran: 1364 A.H./1985.

FVH   *Dhu'l-Riyasitayn, Muhammad. Farhang-i vazhaha-yi ihami dar ash'ar-i Hafez* (*Dictionary of Ambivalent Terms in Hafiz's Verse*). Tehran: Farzan 1379 A.H./2000.

HN   Khurramshahi, Baha al-Din. *Hafez-nama: sharh-i al-faz, i'lam, mafahim-i kilidi va abyat-i dushvar-i Hafez*, 2 vols. Tehran: Intisharat-i Surush 1372 A.H./1993.

HSS   Mu'in, Muhammad. *Hafez-i shirin-sukhan*, 2 vols.
      Tehran: Intisharat-i Mu'in 1370 A.H./1991.

LG   Darabi, Muhammad. *Latifa-yi ghaybi*. Shiraz: Intis-
      harat-i Kitabkhana-yi Ahmadi Shirazi 1357 A.H./1978.

LHI   Browne, E. G. *A Literary History of Persia*, 4 vols.
      Cambridge: Cambridge University Press 1906–30.

LND   Dihkhuda, 'Ali Akbar. *Lughat-nama*, 14 vols., ed. M.
      Mu'in and M. Ja'far Shahidi. Tehran: Mu'assasa-yi
      Lughat-nama Dihkhuda; Tehran University Press 1373
      A.Hsh./1994.

SGH   Haravi, Husayn 'Ali. *Sharh-i ghazalha-yi Hafez*, 4 vols.
      Tehran: Nashr-i Nu 1367 A.H./1988.

SIH   Lahuri, Abu'l-Hasan 'Abd al-Rahman Khatmi. *Sharh-i
      'irfani-yi ghazalha-yi-i Hafez*, 4 vols., ed. Baha al-Din
      Khurramshahi, Kurush Mansuri, and Husayn Muti'i-
      Amin. Tehran: Nashr-i Qatra 1374 A.H./1995.

SNH   Barzigar-Khaliqi, Muhammad Rida. *Shakh-i nabat-i
      Hafez: sharh-i ghazalha, hamrah ba muqaddama,
      talaffaz-i vashigan-i dushvar, durust-khwani-yi abyat
      va farhang-i istilahat-i 'irfani*, 2 vols. Tehran: Zawwar
      1382 A.H./ 2004.

SSH   Sudi Busnawi (of Bosnia), Muhammad. *Sharh-i Sudi
      bar Divan-i Hafez*, trans. Ismat Satarzada, 4 vols., 4th
      ed., Tehran: Intisharat-i Anzali, 1362 A.H./1983.

Notes to the Ghazals

"HOW BLAME HAS BEEN HELPFUL"

Stanza 6: The Persian term translated here as "spot of grief"
is *dagh*, literally meaning "brand," referring to a scorching
hot pain, that sears and "brands" the soul with its red-hot
intensity. *Dagh* may also mean bereavement or remorse. The
heart's *dagh* is thus heart-burning bereavement and heart-
soreness, being the Persian equivalent of St. John of the
Cross's "sweet cautery," exemplifying what Italian poetry in
the Western chivalric tradition called the "passion that brands
the heart."

"MY CLOAK STAINED WITH WINE"

Stanza 6: Khurramshahi (HN, II, pp. 1038–43) correctly
includes this verse among Hafez's great ecstatic paradoxes,
a particular genre of Sufi writing known as *Shath*. Hafez in
the same vein says elsewhere: "Drown yourself for a moment
in God's ocean, yet never imagine that even a hair on your
head will get wet from the waters of all seven seas" (*Divan*, ed.
Khanlari, no. 478, v. 6, cited by Haravi, SGH, III, p. 1732).

Stanza 8: The term "pure wine" (*may-i nab*) refers to romantic human love, engaged in by the lover conditioned by his utter self-abandonment (*'ishq-i majazi mashrut bi-pakbazi*) (SIH, IV, p. 2676).

"THE NIGHT VISIT"

Stanza 5: The reference to Pre-Eternity is to the pre-eternal covenant mentioned in the Koran VII 172. The image of these dregs (of the wine) of this covenant of Pre-Eternity plays on the double entendre of the word: "yes" (*bala*), connoting both "yes" and "calamity."

Stanza 6: An allusion to the doctrine of predestination: whatever God decreed—be it well or ill, balm or wound, sacred or profane—we did.

"THE WORLD IS NOT ALL THAT GREAT"

Stanza 3: The Sidra, or lote tree, is mentioned in the Qur'an (LIII: 13) as part of a heavenly scene in paradise beheld by the Prophet, situated "next to the Garden of the Abode" in the seventh heaven. The Tuba tree is also mentioned in the Qur'an (XIII: 6) as part of the flora of paradise. *Tuba* means blessedness, happiness, and by extension denotes a tree of fortune.

Stanza 8: The very anticlerical doctrine that Hafez preaches in this verse, which equates the inspired libertine with the self-satisfied puritan, can ultimately be directly traced back to the parable of the Pharisee and the Publican in the Gospel of Luke (18:10–14).

"DO NOT SINK INTO SADNESS"

Stanza 1: An allusion to the story of Joseph and his father, Jacob, in the Qur'an (XII: 84). According to later commentators on the Qur'an, Jacob was said to have wept over his separation from Joseph in the "House of Grief" (*bayt al-khazan* in Arabic). In general, in Sufi poetry Joseph figures as an exemplar of the beloved, and Jacob a symbol of the lover suffering in separation from him.

"THE PEARL ON THE OCEAN FLOOR"

Stanza 1: These "dawn studies" refer to lessons, usually in the Qur'an, theology, Arabic humanistic studies, or grammar that Muslim clerics engage in before setting down to the normal business of the day.

Stanza 6: "At the bottom of the ocean can be found the pearl of divine love, which is worth—and even excels in value—all the voyaging which the body makes in its aimless journeys through life. If the soul seeks that unique pearl, found in an oyster in the ocean depths, why should the body just keep on going?" (SIH, IV, p. 2383).

"SAY GOOD-BYE. IT WILL SOON BE OVER."

Stanza 6: Hafez's reference is to the month of Shaban, the eighth Arabic lunar month, which is followed by the month of Ramadan, a month of hyper-orthodox religious devotion and fasting, during which wine (not to mention food and drink from dawn to dusk) must not be consumed.

"THE MAN WHO ACCEPTS BLAME"

Stanza 7: "Thus, the Prophet's invocation: 'I seek refuge in God from useless knowledge . . .'" (SIH, IV, pp. 2564–65).

Stanza 9: Lahuri says: "It is a grave error to kiss the hand of and pledge oneself to those who sell their ascetic abstinence for the sake of riches, worldly rank, and status" (SIH, IV, p. 2566). Khurramshahi cites Imam 'Ali's (d. 40/660) dictum: "Do not kiss the hand of anyone except the hand of a woman by way of sensual passion (*shahwat*) or a child by way of compassion (*rahmat*)" (HN, II, p. 1097).

"THE WINE MADE BEFORE ADAM"

Stanza 5: The "wine made before Adam" here refers to the pre-eternal covenant (*ahd-i alast*) mentioned in the Qur'an (VII: 172), in which God asks the yet uncreated souls of Adam's offspring, "Am I not your Lord?" (*Alastu bi-rabbikum?*) In this unconscious and uncreated state, they all ecstatically and drunkenly reply, "Yes!"

"CONVERSATION WITH THE TEACHER"

Stanza 1: Jamshid was a mythological Iranian king of the Pishdadian dynasty, known for his marvelous cup or goblet (*jam-i jam*), by gazing into which he could behold all the affairs of his kingdom. Jamshid's cup was also known as the "world-revealing goblet" (*jam-i jahan-nama*), and Muslim mythmakers ascribed a similar cup to the prophet Solomon. Occasionally authors have interpreted this cup to mean a kind of mirror that worked as a crystal ball.

Stanza 6: "Our friend" refers here to the Sufi martyr Mansur al-Hallaj (d. 922). The making of the gallows' step seem high probably alludes to Hallaj's illustrious quip on the way to the gallows as narrated by 'Attar in his *Memoirs of the Saints* (*Tadhkira al-awliya'*): "When they brought him [Hallaj] to the base of the gallows at Bab al-Taq, he kissed the wood and set his foot on the ladder. "How do you feel?" they taunted him. "The ascension of true men is to the top of the gallows," he answered (SGH, I, p. 607). The Sufi master Shibli (d. 945), a close friend of the martyred Sufi, was said to have heard a divine voice inform him that Hallaj's sin was to have revealed the mysteries, whence the Sufi maxim "The revelation of the secrets of Lordship is heresy," to which saying the tavern master here alludes (HN, I, p. 571).

Stanza 7: Jesus is portrayed in the Qur'an (II: 87, 254) as being confirmed and supported by the Holy Spirit. In Persian Sufi poetry, poets such as Mahmud Shabistari (d. after 1340) depicted him as the archetype of human spirituality, being himself the *spiritus dei*, or Holy Spirit (cf. Qur'an, IV: 171).

"GABRIEL'S NEWS"

Stanza 4: The lote tree (Sidra) mentioned in the Qur'an (LIII: 13) stands "next to the Garden of the Abode," where it is depicted as part of a heavenly scene beheld by the Prophet. See also "The World Is Not All That Great," note to stanza 3.

"ONE ROSE IS ENOUGH"

Stanza 3: The ascetic relies on his own efforts in the material realm to reach what he imagines to be Paradise, whereas the lover (*'ashiq*) and inspired libertine have long ago abandoned the longing for anything except the divine Beloved. Therefore, both the lover and the inspired libertine have already entered the realm of Paradise by virtue of following their higher *secta amoris*, expressed in this verse by the symbol of the (Magian) tavern.

Stanza 6: An allusion to the Qur'an: "He is with you wheresoever ye are" (LVII: 4).

"REAPING WHEAT"

The ideas, imagery, meter, and rhyme in this ghazal derive from ghazals by Nizari Quhistani and Khwaju Kirmani.

Stanza 1: A reference to this Qur'anic verse: "Each soul earns only its own account, nor can anyone laden down bear another's load" (VI: 164) (SIH, I, p. 546).

Stanza 2: An allusion to the *hadith* of the Prophet: "This world is farmland of the Next" (LG, p. 85). The first two stanzas of the poem loosely paraphrase this Qur'anic verse: "O believers! You are in charge of your own souls. Someone who is a sinner cannot injure you if you are rightly guided" (V: 105) (SGH, I, p. 364; HN, p. 395).

Stanza 5: A reference to the Qur'an: "No calamity befalls you on the earth or in your soul but it has been already inscribed in a Book aforehand . . . so that [knowing this] you do not grieve over what you have missed, nor brag about you have been given" (LVII: 22–23).

"WHAT DO WE REALLY NEED?"

Stanza 3: The polarity between Servant and Lord, Pauper and Prince, and Beggar and King found in this verse is omnipresent throughout Hafez's *Divan*. The "destitute and beggarly person" (*gida* = beggar) here is used only metaphorically to mean a materially destitute pauper. In reality, when Hafez calls himself a beggar, he refers to the idea that he belongs to the company of the "spiritually poor" (*gida* = *faqir*), that is, asserting himself to be a gnostic who is contented and resigned to God's will and who needs nothing but God (that is the exact sense and subject of the next verse) (SGH, I, p. 108).

Stanza 4: Hafez's idiom "lords of owning nothing" (*arbab-i hajat*, lit. "lords of need," or "possessed of dire need") is equivalent to the Gospel phrase "poor in spirit."

Stanza 6: The term translated here as "Solomon's cup" is *jam-i jahan-nama* (the world-displaying goblet), referred to by Hafez in a number of other ghazals in this book.

Stanza 9: The "false face" or "false claimant" (*muda'i*) is the imposter who "falsely lays claims."

"THE ANGELS AT THE TAVERN DOOR"

Stanza 1: The term "last night" *(dush)* refers to four verses of the Qur'an (XXXII: 4–7, and particularly to verses 6 and 7: "(6) Such is He who knows what is hidden and what is evident, the Almighty, the Merciful, (7) who made all things good that He created, and who made man of clay." The reference to kneading Adam's clay alludes to the Prophet's "sacred tradition" (*hadith-i qudsi*) as well: "I [God] kneaded the clay of Adam for forty days and nights" (SIH, II, p. 1179). "The reason why the poet uses the term 'last night' is because the event of human creation from the Wine of Love appears to be as recent as 'last night' to the perfect Sufis" (SIH, II, p. 1178).

The images of the first three stanzas of this ghazal are based on chapter 4 of Najm al-Din Razi's (d. 654/1256) *Mirsad al-'ibad* (HN, I: 677), in whose poetic imagery the divine workshop is depicted as a vast tavern where the angels have brought the clay of Adam to the divine Vintner in order to knead it into the shape of man, which God then "perfected into a beautiful form" (Qur'an XL: 64). The angels, who precede man in the order of being, have entered the tavern/workshop of being, having been given by God the task of pouring his clay into the mold of the 'human form divine'" (SGH, II, pp. 766–67).

Stanza 3: This verse is a paraphrase of the Qur'an: "We offered the trust to the heavens and the earth and the hills, but they shrank from bearing it and were afraid of it, but man assumed it. Lo! he has turned out to be a tyrant and an idiot!" (XXXIII: 73) Hafez's verb "could not bear" is a direct Persian translation of the Arabic original of "but they shrank from bearing . . . " in the Qur'an (SGH, II, p. 769).

Stanza 4: An allusion to this *hadith* of the Prophet: "Verily, after me my community will be subdivided into seventy-three different sects, out of which one will be saved, and the seventy-two others will be in hell."

"DECIDING NOT TO GO TO INDIA"

According to Edward Browne (LHP, III, p. 285; also repeated by Khanlari in his notes to the *Divan*, II, pp. 1193–95), legend has it that this ghazal was composed after Hafez had accepted the invitation of Mahmud Shah Bahmani of the Deccan to visit his court, having traveled to the Persian Gulf for this purpose. However, while waiting at Hormuz for the ship, such a storm rose that he decided to call off the voyage.

"THE WIND IN SOLOMON'S HANDS"

Stanza 1: The "First Covenant with Adam" here refers to the pre-eternal covenant (*ahd-i alast*) mentioned in the Qur'an, in which God asks the yet uncreated souls of Adam's offspring, "Am I not your Lord?" (*Alastu bi-rabbikum?*). In this unconscious and uncreated state, they all ecstatically and drunkenly reply, "Yes! We bear witness to it" (*bala shahidna*) (VII: 172). In the case of Hafez (see ghazals 21: 1; 22: 5; 26: 10; 107: 5), this pre-eternal intoxication, symbolic of the rapture of divine attraction that pulls man to God, has still not diminished (SGH, I, p. 629). See also the note on "The Wine Made Before Adam."

Stanza 2: The reference here is to the four recitations (*char takbir*) of *Allah akbar* ("God is great") recited over a cadaver during Muslim funeral prayers according to the Sunni rite (HN, I, pp. 209–10).

Stanza 4: The poet compares the place of nature ("mountain") unfavorably to that of man ("ant"), the "mountain" here being referred to in this Qur'anic verse: "We offered the trust unto the heavens and the earth and the *mountains*, but they shrank from bearing it and were afraid of it. And man assumed it. Lo! He has proved a tyrant and a fool" (XXXIII: 72). "Hafez proceeds to reveal 'the mystery of Fate' he had mentioned in the previous line, revealing that in the World of Love, the strength and endurance of the withers of an ant— symbol of poor, weak-willed man—is greater than that of the withers of a mountain. He declares that 'Although there are powers in nature that are supreme and superior to man—such as the mountains—yet even the mountains shrank from bearing the weight of the heavenly trust that man accepted.' Man therefore has a greater power to absorb wisdom than all other forces of nature, and so he is all the more worthy to receive divine love" (SGH, I, p. 245). Hafez's injunction not to despair is inspired by this passage from the Qur'an: "Do not despair of the Holy Spirit. No one but those who reject the truth despair of the Holy Spirit" (XII: 87).

Stanza 7: According to the Qur'an, the wind was at the beck and call of Solomon's royal will.

"RECITING THE OPENING CHAPTER"

This is one of Hafez's most celebrated ghazals devoted to the theme of "music, moody food of us that trade in love . . ." (*Anthony and Cleopatra*, II.5). Several lines of this ghazal (especially 1–2; 7–9) have become household adages in Persian in the treasury of famous Hafez quotations.

Stanza 4: The term "majesty" in Persian is *Farr*, an Avestan and Pahlavi word referring to the imperial glory of the ancient Iranian kings (G. Gnoli, "Farr[ah]," *Encyclopedia Iranica*,

IX, pp. 312–19). The lover likens his poor, wretched passion to that of the lowest of flying creatures, the fly, for sugar, and the beloved's requiting of this passion with the condition of the "king of the birds," the fabulous mythological Huma (sometimes identified with the osprey or phoenix). In Persian mythology, it is said that upon whomever the shadow of the Huma's plume fell would become endowed with the "royal fortune" of a king.

"BECOME A LOVER"

Stanza 2: Hafez's verse is probably influenced by the medieval idea that weakened physical powers increase the sight of the soul (cf. Craig, *The Enchanted Glass*, 1936, pp. 45–46).

Stanza 3: In this couplet Hafez provides an exact versification of a saying by the Sufi saint Shah Shuja' Kirmani (d. after 270/884) concerning the true meaning of "learning" (*fadl*): "Learned and intellectual folk (*ahl-i fadl*) may be said to be more virtuous than other people as long as they do not see their own learning, but once they perceive themselves to be learned or virtuous, they cease to have any virtue at all" ('Attar, *Tadhkirat al-awliya'*, ed. M. Isti'lami, 6th ed., Tehran, 1370 A.H./1991, p. 379).

Stanza 5: "Whoever realizes love in the world will keep this quality as his friend down into the tomb. So the poet enjoins one to take advantage of the few days of life given in the world, to make use of them to become a lover and to practice love, which virtue alone will remain with one forever and permanently unto all eternity. The lover alone knows how to decipher the purpose of God's creation. In the *Kashf al-mahjub*, it is related, 'Tomorrow when a line is crossed through all the ordinances of the Canon Law, only these two things will survive into eternity: one is love and the other gratitude for love, for 'an atom of love is better than seventy years of worship'" (SIH, IV, p. 2861).

"THE DUST OF THE DOORWAY"

Stanza 1: The term "secret Witness" (*shahid*) is a very important word in Hafez's poetry. The *shahid* is something found to be acceptable to the eyes of the heart, bearing "witness" to God's handiwork. Because the soul is dominated by passions (*nafs-i ammara*), the heart is unable to apprehend reality. So in its pursuit of this "invisible witness of beauty" (*shahid-i ghaybi*), the seeker's heart attaches itself to a form in this visible phenomenal world, which it hankers after instead. If that pursuit takes the seeker to a higher realm, it is a good step, but if the *shahid* takes him to a lower realm, it is not so good. The greedy soul doesn't want to attach itself to the divine, so it will attach itself to a "pretty face" or some other image that attracts it. So whatever the mystic's heart hangs upon, whether this be a phenomenal form (*surat*), a song (*awaz*), a verse, an idea, or a moment of meditation, is his *shahid* (FAH, p. 361). Yeats, in his poem "Memory," thus writes:

One had a lovely face,
And two or three had charm,
But charm and face were in vain
Because the mountain grass
Cannot but keep the form
Where the mountain hare has lain.

"GOBBLING THE SUGAR OF DAWN SLEEP"

Stanza 1: In Khanlari's edition of the *Divan*, instead of "the existence of love" (*hasti-yi 'ishq*), the phrase "drunkenness of love" (*masti-yi 'ishq*) is given. The former reading that we have chosen here is more authentic (it is featured in six of Khanlari's variant MSS.); furthermore, "the existence of love" is also the preferred reading of both Haravi and Khurramshahi, and Khanlari's arguments for "drunkenness" (*Divan*, II, pp. 1225–26) are convincingly refuted by Haravi. This couplet is usually considered by most commentators to be a paraphrase of the verse: "I did not create the jinn and human beings except for the sake of worship of Me" (Qur'an, LI: 56). Man has been created so that he/ she may become a lover. The difference between man and the angel lies in the fact that angels have no love, whereas men cannot live without love (SGH, III, p. 1827).

Stanza 5: Since all the commentators agree that this is a Sufi mystical ghazal, they rightly explain the "kingdom" spoken of here as being the "kingdom of spiritual poverty."

Stanza 6: In this couplet, like the previous one, the poet uses ethical and metaphysical arguments as tactics of seduction to further his erotic advances. He entreats his beloved to favor him with a glance out of the "corner" of her eye to avoid becoming subject to any untoward calamity (the glance from the corner of the eyes is juxtaposed, both by poetic device and alliteration, to "recluses" who sit in corners). The term *bala*, translated here as "disaster," refers to the adversities, troubles, or disasters that afflict mankind, which, according to traditional Islamic (and Christian) piety, can be averted by sincere prayer, as Blake's stanzas (from "The Grey Monk") indicate:

> But vain the Sword & vain the Bow.
> They can never work War's overthrow.
> The hermit's prayer and widow's tear
> Alone can save the world from fear.
>
> For a Tear is an Intellectual Thing,
> And a Sigh is the Sword of an Angel King,
> And the bitter groan of the Martyr's woe
> Is an Arrow from the Almightie's Bow.

"ABOUT DESTITUTE LOVERS"

Stanza 2: Khurramshahi (HN, II, p. 1166–87) has a long discussion of the varieties of love in Hafez's *Divan*, where he notes that there are some thirty-eight different characteristics of love, citing some fourteen different couplets in which love and reason are opposed to each other, one of which is this verse (HN, II, pp. 1182–83), He also devotes a long discussion to the love/reason dichotomy in his commentary on two other ghazals (HN, I, pp. 754–56; 689–92). He concludes that "the opposition of reason (*'aql*) and love is just like the opposition of two completely different perspectives or movements, each of which has been intensely powerful in the history of human thought. The first is philosophy or rational, demonstrative science, which is the Peripatetic school going back to Aristotle, and the second is the philosophy of love and vision, which is the Ishraqi school, originating in Plato. Naturally Hafez, like the Sufi mystics (*'urafa*), supports and cherishes love, which he refuses to relinquish" (HN, I, p. 692).

Stanza 3: The poet compares the tight pursed lips of his beloved to the signet ring of the Supreme King, whose stamp (i.e., her lips) rules the world. In the Sufi tradition, it is often said that the world is subject to the sway of the mystic who knows the "Supreme Name" *(ism-i a'zam)* of God. The ring of Solomon apparently had this name printed on it so that he dominated the world by power of that ring.

Stanza 6: Referring to the *hadith* of the Prophet: "The *faqir* is seated beside God on the Day of Resurrection'" (SIH, III, p. 1613).

Stanza 7: An allusion to Qur'an LXVIII: 17–33, which tells the story of a group of gardeners who refused to give to the poor the leftovers of their harvest, as a consequence of which God destroyed their entire garden.

Stanza 9: "Within this phrase lies the idea that it is proper that princes and paupers be seated side by side because 'things through their opposites are best comprehended,' and hence the adage: 'The beggar's cry gives honor to the market-place of the generous'" (SIH, III, pp. 1614–15).

"THE ONE WHO REMAINS DISGRACED"

Stanza 1: In his *Subtleties of the Invisible Realm,* a Sufi commentary on the *Divan* of Hafez, Muhammad Darabi paraphrases this line's symbolism, saying that the face signifies the light of the divine Essence, a radiant ray of which appears reflected in the cup of the wine, a symbol for the poet's illuminated heart. The human being who is subject to this illumination immaturely believes that the light has come from himself and not from God (LG, p. 75).

Stanza 2: "The beauty of the Eternal Beloved manifested itself but once—creating Love, Lover, and all else. Although He was pure Unity and Oneness, and only One can proceed from One, in the fanciful mind of man preoccupied with multiplicity, various images appeared. In other words, Hafez states that multiplicity is purely fanciful and imaginary, not real. What is authentically *real* is that unique 'ray of splendour' and peerless divine Beauty" (HN, I, p. 485).

Stanza 4: "This line alludes to Love's overwhelming domination [of the lover]. As the adage [of Junayd] goes: 'The tongue of whoever knows God falls silent'" (LG, pp. 82–83).

Stanza 5: The "mosque" here symbolizes pharisaical piety, ascetic discipline without love, and conventional Shari'a-oriented legalism, contrasted to the tavern of ruin (*kharabat*) symbolic of the higher religion of love (HN, I, p. 487). "Muhammad Parsa said: 'Whoever does not go to the Tavern is irreligious / Since the Tavern is the basis of Religion'" (SIH, II, pp. 1428–29). The pre-eternal "agreement" refers to Qur'an VII: 172.

Stanza 7: An allusion to this tale about Hallaj from 'Attar's *Tadhkira al-awliya'*: On his way to the gallows, "Hallaj strutted proudly along the road bravely gesturing with his arms like a tough brigand. 'What is this proud gait all about?' he was asked. 'It is because I am going to slaughterhouse,' he replied" (SGH, I, pp. 472–73). Being slain by the divine Beloved, the lover thus enjoys a "good situation" (SIH, II, p. 1432).

Stanza 11: The term "game of glances" (*nazar-bazi*) means

110

"playing with one's glance," "to cast a flirtatious glance upon," "to capriciously regard mortal beauty," which is "a key term in the poetry of Hafez, and an art of particular significance to him, of which he boasts in many verses" (HN, I, pp. 705–6).

"THE GUESTHOUSE WITH TWO DOORS"

Stanza 1: The phrase "Sufis who love each moment" (*Sufiyan-i waqt-parast*) amounts to a call to joy. The poet praises one who acts according to the dictates of the present moment in total disregard to all prior precedent and reason and also one who enjoys and takes advantage of the present moment, and considers past and future with an equal mind" (FVH, p. 425). In the Four Quartets, Eliot also uses the symbol of the rose to represent the "eternal moment": "The moment of the rose and the moment of the yew tree / Are of equal duration. A people without history / Is not redeemed from time, for history is a pattern / Of timeless moments" (Little Gidding, IV).

Stanza 2: It was the custom for the Sufis to smash wineglasses on a rock and thus "lay down the foundation" of their firm conversion and repentance to God. Hafez ironically inverts this practice with sarcasm here, punning on the idea that it is the repentance as firm and hard as rock that should have broken the glasslike cup—not vice versa (SNH, pp. 67–68).

Stanza 3: Since God is the All-Wealthy (*al-Ghani*), He has no need of man's obedience and worship, and thus worldly rank and position are held to be of no account: whether dissolute drunkard or pious hermit, all are weighed in the same balance (SGH, I, p. 240).

Stanza 5: The souls binding themselves in Pre-Eternity here refers to the pre-eternal covenant (*ahd-i alast*) mentioned in Qur'an VII: 172 (see "The Wind in Solomon's Hands," pp. 43–44). The souls' affirmation of "yes" during this covenant contains a double entendre, since "yes" in Arabic (*bala*) also means "calamity." Annemarie Schimmel explains that in this Qur'anic passage "the theme of Affliction, *bala'*, is ingeniously combined with the word *bala*, 'yes,' that the souls spoke at the Day of the Covenant, thus accepting in advance every tribulation that might be showered upon them until Doomsday" (*Mystical Dimensions of Islam* [Chapel Hill: University of North Carolina Press, 1975], pp. 136–37).

Stanza 6: An allusion to Qur'an: "Everything is perishing but His Face" (XXVIII: 88; SNH, p. 69).

Stanza 7: According to the Qur'an (XXI: 81; XXVII:16), the winds were at Solomon's beck and call and he understood the speech of the birds.

"SOME ADVICE"

Stanza 2: The "great bird" mentioned here is the 'Anqa, a fabulous bird in Persian mythology equivalent to the Simurgh of 'Attar's *Conference of the Birds*, whose nest is on Mount Qaf, a mountain chain that, in Persian mythology, encircles the entire world. In 'Attar's poem, the "Bird of Solomon," or hoopoe (mentioned in the Qur'an, XXVII: 22–26), was the guide of all the thirty birds seeking the Simurgh, through whose intercession the poet says he was able to traverse and complete all the stages of the spiritual life (HN, I, p. 931).

Stanza 4: This line is inspired by a verse by the Persian poet Nizami (d. 598/1202) that maintains, "Whatever befalls you contrary to your habit is the caravan leader of Felicity," and another line of similar purport by Kamal Khujandi (d. 803/1400): "Her disheveled curls are a cause of our inner collectedness and concentration. Since this is the case, then one must make the curls even more disheveled." "In most mystical texts, the key to reaching one's goal is said to lie in opposition to the lower soul's (*nafs*) habitual ways and customs. . . . In fact, doing things by normal rote and habit is considered to indicate spiritual negligence" (*ghiflat*) (HN, I, p. 932).

Stanza 5: "Wherever the word 'treasure' (*ganj*) occurs in Persian poetry, it is nearly always followed by the word 'ruin' (*virana*), since treasures are normally found in ruins" (SGH, II, p. 1321).

Stanza 10: "The *mihrab* is the highest place in a mosque which faces the *qibla*, the direction of prayer pointing towards Mecca, consisting of a niche with an highly decorated arch or dome, supporting columns and capitals, in the shallow recess or which the Imam (prayer leader) stands during congregational prayer, similar to the Jewish synagogue's apse that is oriented towards Jerusalem" (G. Fehérvári, "Mihrab," in *Encyclopedia of Islam*, 2nd ed., VII, pp. 7–15).

"A GLASS OF WINE"

Stanza 2: A reference to the Prophet's *hadith*: "Travel lightly like the solitary wayfarer." This saying of the early Sufi saint Hasan Basri, "Those who traveled lightly were saved, and those with heavy burdens perished" (Hujwiri, *Kashf al-*

mahjub, ed. Zhukovskii [St. Petersburg, 1899; reprinted, Leningrad, 1926], p. 472), should also be cited here.

Stanza 7: The "wine of Pre-Eternity" (*bada azal*) refers to the wine drunk in eternity before time (see also "The Wine Made Before Adam" and "The Wind in Solomon's Hands"). Lahuri explains this verse in the traditional context of drunken Sufis as follows: "Long before Adam had attained to existence, this company of Sufis were completely out of their wits and senses, drunkenly circling the Holy House" (SIH, I, p. 349).

"ON THE WAY TO THE GARDEN"

This ghazal is modeled after a ghazal in the same meter and rhyme by the Isma'ili poet Nizari Quhistani (d. 721/1321), many of the ideas and imagery of which were appropriated by Hafez for his own purposes.

Stanza 3: *Urdibihisht,* translated as "May" here, is the second month of the Persian solar calendar, beginning in mid-April and ending mid-May. Being in its harmony and equilibrium a manifestation of Paradise, *Urdibihisht* is considered to be the most "heavenly" month, which makes it also doctrinally correct for the meadow to tell "the simple tale" of this "heavenly" month.